The Legend of the

Christmas Queen

THE LEGEND OF THE CHRISTMAS QUEEN

Copyright Henrik Neergaard 2021

Published by Books-on-Demand Publishing House, Copenhagen Denmark

Printed by Books-on-Demand Publishing House, Norderstedt, Germany

ISBN 9788743032991

Henrik Neergaard

The Legend of the Christmas Queen

Books-on-Demand
Publishing House

The background

Some years ago, when I was younger, I was studying at the university in the town of B**** in my home country. I had been engaged to a beautiful young girl from a prosperous and respectable family in the neighboring country N*****, who was admittedly bigger and more powerful than my own country of birth, but in many respects also more primitive, since it was not only poor, but also subject to a brutal and dictatorial regime.

During the Christmas holidays of the following events, I was scheduled to visit my fiancée's parents for the first time and spend Christmas with them so that we could get to know each other. I hadn't previously visited the country N****. I knew it only by the news, from newspaper reading and watching television, and was therefore excited about what awaited me. And most of all, to meet with my fiancé after a period of one long year, where we had only been in contact by means of writing letters, after she had returned to her parents in her hometown. And of course, I was very excited, and even a bit nervous about meeting her parents.

My fiancé was J**** and for a couple of semesters, she had been a visiting student at the university in my hometown, where I also studied. That's how we'd met and had gotten to know each other. About one year ago, however, she had returned to her homeland. She had quite suddenly been called home by her parents, without the reason for it really being clear to me. But it was probably related to the fact that her father had been required to take a job change by the regime. Whether he had been promoted to a more important kind of job, or, on the contrary, demoted, was not apparent from my fianc é e's often rather succinct but very loving letters to me. All this took place a few decades ago, when letter writing was still the natural way to stay in touch over longer distances.

My fianc é and her parents lived in the town of P****, which was the country's second largest city. It was even more than the capital V**** marked by steel mills, blast furnaces, coal mines and other heavy industry. At the same time, however, it was a million-inhabitants city with a university and other higher education institutions. My fianc é had just passed a final exam on her studies at the city university.

Her father was the director of one of the steel works in the city and thus belonged to the privileged upper class in the country. Her mother was the principal of a high school. I hadn't met any of her parents or other family members before, so I was excited about what this year's Christmas commemoration would be like. I had heard rumors, that there were to be quite a few old and more distinctive Christmas traditions in this country, without being able to know what exactly they were about. I think it should even be more pronounced in the town of P****, which was reportedly in the most old-fashioned and backward part of the country, where the archaic traditions had apparently stayed the longest.

The town of P**** was far out at the opposite end of the country compared to the capital city of V****, in a mountain area, with land that was rocky and hard to cultivate, and really only had a little grazing for sheep and goats. As a result, the population of this whole part of the country had been among the poorest and most backward in the whole region. However, the area was rich in coal, lignite, iron ore and a number of other metals and minerals, including lead, copper, zinc and others. As a result, within about 100 years, the city had evolved from a small mountain town into a busy and noisy and heavily polluted industrial town.

Today it was still the center of the country's mining and steel industry and housed both blast furnaces, steel mills and a large number of large factories, especially in the production of machinery and other heavy industries such as railway equipment, tractors, belt vehicles, tanks and a large arms industry, which was mainly supplied to the country's own oversized military, but reportedly also had some exports to light-shade buyers in many places abroad.

I had read about all this in advance. Moreover, most of it was well known as general knowledge in my home country, which was both smaller, more prosperous, modern and with a more democratic form of government than in the large neighboring country of N****, which I was about to visit during the Christmas holidays.

The city of P**** was, incidentally, the hometown of the country's dictator Augusto Miranka. It was the city where the country's longtime sole ruler was born and raised, and it was said that he greatly favored the city and gave it special advantages, just as he often preferred to stay there rather than in the capital city.

He was now in his late fifties and had ruled the country with a heavy hand for about 30 years. Before him, there had been a number of other rulers of roughly the same sort. Some of them, including Miranka himself, had tried to cast a tinge of democracy over the regime, but without any realities in it. It was just a sham democracy with staged presidential elections, massive propaganda, state-run media and fierce prosecution of dissidents and political opponents.

Visitors from abroad, on the other hand, was generally welcomed, as the regime was trying to build a tourism industry that could inject much-needed foreign currency into the poor country. So I had no qualms about visiting the country, all the more so since I had been invited by my fiancée's father, who was, after all, a steelworks director and had to be considered as a high ranking member of society.

This was all just to describe the background to the events that were going to take place during the following days. A very special Christmas period, which I think I will always remember. In the following attempt to write down the events that took place in these few days, I rely on the diary I kept during my stay in the city of P**** in the country N**** during the Christmas holidays that year, and therefore the narrative changes over to the present, just like in my diary entries.

My arrival to the city

I had arrived in the city of P**** by train. A journey that would normally take somewhere between 9 and 10 hours from my hometown in the neighboring country. But the train is delayed, both because of some track work, but also on the grim of heavy snowfall. There have been several lengthy stops along the way, and a few times the train has been diverted along a different and longer route, just as it has been running at a reduced speed.

All this means that I do not arrive in the city of P**** until about an hour and a half after midnight. It means, of course, that it's far too late to go to my fianc é's family now. I was otherwise invited to have dinner with them, the special kind of Christmas dinner, which I have been told is an important tradition in this country. I am somewhat concerned that I have not even been able to notify them along the way and explain why I have been delayed. But it has been impossible to access a usable phone along the way, even though I have tried several times. But now it's long past midnight, and all there is to do is find a hotel room where I can get a good night's sleep on top of the long and strenuous train journey.

It turns out to be all the luck that there is a hotel almost right next to the railway station. It looks quite run down and dilapidated from the point of view of the street, but it turns out that they have not closed for the night as I first thought because there was dark in the windows to the restaurant and the other places. After ringing the night bell and waiting a few minutes, I managed to get the door open and have my luggage dragged to the counter at the reception. The receptionist is sitting sleeping with his head resting on a newspaper located on the counter. He snores loudly, but after several attempts I manage to get him awakened. He asks me to write my name to be registered in the hotel book, where there are several boxes to fill in.

Then he finds five or six other paper forms from a shelf under the counter. A few of them are on several pages with many small boxes that need to be carefully filled in. The receptionist studies them carefully, looks at me, then he shrugs his shoulders and archives the forms in separate folders after first having duly stamped and countersigned them next to my signature.

After all this paperwork is done, I get a room up on the third floor. He rings a bell to summon someone to carry my luggage. After trying in vain several times, at last an old, skinny and worn-out looking maid shows up, apparently also acting as a luggage carrier. She's dresses in an old and rather curly black dress that hangs around her body and seems to be much too big. She laboriously drags my luggage up to my room on the third floor. Despite my protestations that I can take the largest of the suitcases myself. After all, I'm bigger, stronger and younger than her.

We have to climb a pretty steep staircase. Apparently, there's no elevator, or it doesn't work. On my question about it, she just mutters something incomprehensible, and it doesn't get any better when I ask her to repeat it.

When we've got to get to the 3rd floor, we're going to have to go down a long hallway before we get to the room assigned to me. The old maid drags my suitcases into the room and gives herself time to make my bed, fetch towels for the bath, and other things of this kind. Apparently, the bed must first be cleaned up after the previous guest, now that they have had the room rented out for the night. It does not seem like there are very many guests in the hotel.

I ask if there is a telephone somewhere, I can borrow so I can call my future father-in-law and explain why I have been delayed and did not show up for dinner as I was invited. I have come to think that a prominent man like him, who is the director of one of the city's largest steel works, probably has a voicemail where I can leave a short message so I don't chase him out of bed in the middle of the night. I feel

17

obliged to explain why and how I has been delayed.

(I all took place some decades ago, before the invention of cell phones).

The maid shows me to an old-fashioned payphone at the other end of the long walk. Fortunately, she can also exchange one of my banknotes in the country's currency, so I can get some coins to make a call for. I cross my fingers, hoping that it is an answering machine that I connect to, and fortunately that turns out to be the case too.

I'm just going to leave a brief message about the rather embarrassing situation. I can't help making sure the train was delayed along the way. But it's still an unfortunate start to meeting his future in-laws. And even at Christmas.

Meanwhile, the maid has stood either side and probably heard everything I've said. Well, there's nothing to hide either. Now she's following me back to my hotel room. She's finished getting it ready for the night, as far as I can tell. But suddenly she's approaching. Asking for a fee. Not just a small tip like the waiter in a restaurant. Rather like some kind of prostitute, that is. I am confused. I refuse. But she keeps going. She repeats her offer and mentions a price that I could well afford. But I just don't want her.

She insists. Apparently, she does not understand, why I do not want to buy her for the night. She keeps insisting. She says that's what all the male hotel guests do. She makes it sound like I am abnormal and weird because I'm not taking her offer. I am tired after the long journey and I do not fancy her at all. I tell her that I am not

19

interested. She goes on. I ask her to shut up.

In an almost whining voice, she asks why I don't want to help her. She begins on a longer explanation about the background to it. She can hear that I come from another country. What she's telling me shocks me quite a bit. The employment conditions in that country sound absolutely insane and highly offensive to employees, if that is really true.

She says that she is very poor and that her family is hard hit by unemployment and has no money to spend Christmas for. Besides, the hotelier expects her to do it. And expects that the guest accepts her offer. Otherwise, her salary will be deducted, she says. Every morning, she has to hand over half of the amount she has earned that way to the hotelier. For every male guest who has stayed overnight. Mind you, whether the men bought her as a whore or not. Then she just has to pay the amount herself.

In any case, the host must have the money. It is apparently almost inconceivable that one of the male guests says no to her. And if he does, it's money out of the pocket for her. And her salary as a maid is already so low that you can hardly live on it, she says. There's something in her voice and her whole way of telling me about it that makes me believe what she tells me, even if it sounds crazy.

But it can't be legal for the hotelier to treat his employees that way, I say. But it obviously can be in this country. And that's why every man who spends the night in the hotel usually says yes to it. All men, she repeats. Everyone. If nothing else, to help her, so she is not completely ruined.

If, for instance, there were 10 overnight men in the hotel during a month who said no and wouldn't buy her, then she would have to hand over more money to the hotelier in the morning than a full week's salary, she says. Conversely, she herself would make more money from the ten men if they bought her than she otherwise earns in a week of normal hourly pay.

Something begging has come over her voice, but I'm tired after the journey and don't feel like it. But to help her, I take out the wallet and give her the amount she says that she usually makes so she doesn't lose money on me. It may also be that it's just a trick to coax some extra tips out of foreign tourists, I suddenly think. But it is not a large amount in my home country's currency, so peace be with it, I think, and I say that I would like to give her the amount she usually receives, but without her having to sleep with me.

Then I think the problem should be solved, but no. Because it's against the rules, she says. If she accepts the money, she must also deliver the goods, i.e. some specified kind of sex service. Otherwise, she risks losing her job, or even being punished for it. Then she will be accused of fraud, or of having stolen the money from the hotel guest. One of her colleagues did, she says. She was immediately fired and was even dragged to court, charged with theft. Although she escaped with a suspended sentence, this was only because she gave the male judge a whole range of fairly sophisticated sex services. The laws around money and payment are very strict in this country, she explains.

By contrast, she goes on explaining, prostitution is a perfectly legal profession – provided that the income is shared with a male pimp, who must have at least half of what she earns. In addition, the State must have a specific charge for each customer she has. A kind of VAT, except that it a fixed amount per customer per hour started and per specific sex service completed. In fact, a significant part of the state's revenue comes from this tax on the widely used more or less shady forms of prostitution. Without all that money, the state would go bust, she says. The thousands of unemployed men and women – and their families – would have nothing to live on because there are no trade unions or unemployment benefits. Unions are illegal and everyone must cope with themselves as best they can.

That means that most unemployed men – and many other men, especially among the poorer part of the population, industrial workers and other kinds of underpaid workers – have a wife or girlfriend who supports them in this way. The unemployment rate among working people is very high, and growing.

But there is also a fairly large middle class, mostly bureaucrats and party officials who earn relatively well and are almost secured employment for life. Through the widespread prostitution there is actually an economic redistribution, so that the poorer part of the population, especially the factory workers and the farm workers on the large state-owned farm estates, can still have something to live on, she says. I can hear that it is something that really concerns her, but I am too tired to hear a full lecture on the social conditions in this country, even if it sounds horrific. In did not know from my reading about the country, or from what my fianc é told me, that it was that bad. But I am tired, and I just want to go to bed and sleep.

Once again, I offer her the money she is asking for, but without any kind of sexual services from her. I promise to keep quiet to her boss that she has not provided anything for the money. But no, it doesn't work that way, she says. Because there's video surveillance in every room, and if she's going to take time off with the hotelier, she's going to have to turn on the surveillance so he's got it all on tape and can see that she's not lying about it.

At last I give in and agree to it, even though I don't want to, because she's old and ugly and I'm tired after the trip. But I realize that I'm probably not going to go to bed until I say yes. To my surprise, it turns out that she's an amazing mistress, really refined into the art of lovemaking, and she keeps inciting me over and over again.

As soon as I get here, she starts over so I'm not able to resist her, and every time it like there's a little bell tingling somewhere in the background. Four times. Not in my head, not in my mind, that is not what I mean. Rather like some kind of cash register, probably connected to the hidden video cameras. For accounting reasons. I wonder if she will get higher pay from the hotelier for making me come four times rather than just one. After all, I only paid her for one. Or did she forget to ask for more money? Anyway, I hope that at least she is not deducted in her pay because of this. I do not know how this strange and weird systems works. It could be either way.

After that, she slipped out of bed and away in a matter of seconds, before I could ask her anything about anything. I immediately fell asleep to the sound of her busy steps down the stairs. Maybe there was some other overnight male guest that she got to entertain in the same way. Poor maid.

It's the middle of the afternoon when I finally wake up. I get a jug of coffee and some breakfast brought up to the room, and then I fall asleep again. It's gotten dark outside when I wake up again, and a glance at the clock tells me it's late at night. Damn it, too. I have to call my future father-in-law and excuse me one more time — but what should I come up with as an explanation this time? First, I get another jug of coffee. I need something to wake up right on, and to strengthen myself so I can think of something to explain to my father-in-law. It certainly doesn't look good. I come to meet my fianc é e's parents, and then I'm completely impossed because I've been cheating on my fianc é e and slept with a whore all night. And it is the second day in a row that I have to cancel and explain that I will not be there until tomorrow.

Then I realize that I also need something to eat. I'm starving, I haven't had anything to eat all day, except for some breakfast. I call the old maid, who is apparently the only one of her kind and also do it out for room service in areas other than the nocturnal ones. But she says that in the evening there is only serving down in the restaurant.

Then I go down to the restaurant on the ground floor. It looks just as shabby and run down as the rest of the hotel. There are no other guests in the large empty restaurant where the lights are only on at one end of the room. I am assigned a seat at a table where the hotelier and the maid are also about to start a meal. I wonder if I might be the only guest in the hotel.

I look around a little hesitantly as the more than middle-aged hotelier is commanding his stale wife, who acts as a chef, while an ancient white-haired man who could be the host's father – he looks like him at least – thumps around as a waiter and serves for us.

I ask for a menu card, but the host responds in an unfriendly tone of voice that there is no menu. They only serve the dish of the day. I ask what it is, but only get the answer that it is the dish of the day. As I mentioned, I'm starving, and I order a double portion as a precaution so as not to go to bed hungry if the portions turn out to be as scraped as anything else. It takes a long time before the food arrives. Even if it is the dish of the day, it must apparently first be prepared from the ground up to each order.

In the meantime, the hotelier starts questioning me. First about my background, where I come from, who my family is, what I'm studying, what my

father and mother work with, how many
siblings I have and what they do, why I've
come here, and so on and so on. And he
wants precise details, not just loose talk.
He does not allow himself anything but to
be carefully answered, he drills into each
subject with in-depth questions. It seems
like he's having some practice in that kind
of thing.

Then he goes on to question both the maid
and me in turn about our hot lover's night,
as he consistently calls it. In every detail.
He even takes notes, like during the first
part of "our friendship's sharing of
knowledge,", as he calls it. While he is
constantly studying the cashier's notes
from the reception, where all the amounts
that the maid has settled with him for the
night's activities are deposited. Apparently,
he needs to see if true what I'm telling him
about it. Perhaps he is afraid that during
the night I have cheated myself into some

extra services for which it has not been
properly settled.

The food still hasn't come on the table, but
the hotelier eagerly pours up to both
himself and me of an old dusty bottle with
a slightly thin and rather sour red wine.
Suddenly he turns around and seems to be
in a completely different mood. Now he is
suddenly very jovial and friend-like, even
servile. Like he wants to flatter me. Or as if
I am a distinguished and very welcome
guest.

He also begins to praise the old maid
sitting next to him for her amazing
diligence and skill for everything he can
think of. He praises all her good qualities
in completely exuberant terms. As if he
were the father of a somewhat floral old
maiden of a daughter whom he is eager to
get devoted to a nice and wealthy man of
good family. He obviously sees me as a

good party that he would like her to marry. It's not going to be said straight, but behind all his slandered talk, the meaning is clear enough. The maid just sits there and looks down at the table as if all this makes her feel ashamed. She clearly has nothing to say. I myself am too baffled by the whole situation to think of something sensible to say. The hotelier talks like a waterfall. No one else says anything.

Finally my meal arrives. It turns out that it is very plentiful so it a single portion would have been enough. It's a concoction of some kind that I don't exactly recognize. It tastes fairly okay, and it certainly saturates well. But it's not exactly a culinary treat.

The host continues to pour plenty of the sour, thin red wine, and fills my glass to the brim every time I've taken a few mouthfuls. The food is pretty salty, so I must have something to wash it down with. Dinner pulls out because the host has again started questioning me about all sorts of things. Even some fairly personal things that require some more detailed answers. Otherwise, he'll just keep asking. He's going to get it out of me anyway. I am quite sure of that. He has apparently never been outside the country and he also wants to know all about what it is like in the country I come from.

I understand from what he is saying that television and the radio broadcasts and the newspapers contain virtually only government propaganda and little about what is happening in the world. It sounds somewhat like the Soviet Union or Eastern Europe. In combination with a lot of centuries-old twisted and prejudiced perceptions that constantly shine through most of what he says.

It is almost midnight before the meal is finished. Another day has passed without me managing to reach my future in-laws, who probably can't understand why I haven't turned up. This is a disaster. A very bad start to a relationship. A marriage even. The phone system is still not working after the latest crash, I was told when asked at the reception. Once more, it has also become far too late to call. At the same time, I feel a growing irritation with the hotelier and the whole situation.

Now it's just a matter of getting a good night's sleep, so I'm ready for the next day's challenges and meeting with my in-laws and my fianc é e. I'm sure she can't understand where I'm going. I must find a way to explain all this.

Rather intoxicated by all the bad red wine and with my stomach full of too much heavy food, I stagger up the stairs to my hotel room. The maid follows after me and sets up a new love night similar to the previous one. I'm tired and I just want to sleep. I don't want her at all. But she's going to keep on trying to persuade me, no matter what I say. Finally, I give in, just to get it over with and get rid of her torment. But I'm missing every fiery. I try to think about my fiancé in the meantime, but it is no success. The difference is far too big. And I do not want to be cheating on her.

Eventually I fell asleep in the middle of it all. Fortunately. I was afraid she'd keep me awake all night. I wonder what it means for her settlement with the host when I fell asleep without ending it. I think this kind of thing is a very relevant question in this country. There are security cameras in every room, so everything is filmed. I later found out why. There is an extensive industry and all this footage from the surveillance cameras is being sold to some

companies that cut it together for some
movies. Not just from hotel rooms, but also
from all the other places where prostitution
or half-prostitution is going on.

Apparently they've cultivated a market for
this kind of porn abroad, so the movies are
sold across most of the world as one of
the few export goods they can earn any
foreign currency on. It has become an
important source of income for many
people to sell these recordings to one of
the numerous companies, the largest of
which are state-owned, at least officially.
In reality, they are owned by the dictator
and his family. But it was only later, after I
had met with some dissidents, that I got to
know all this.

The next day I slept until well into the
morning. Ate a modest lunch. Tried to call
my fiancé and her parents, but the
telephone network was still down. Then I

started packing my things and got ready to finally leave the old, run-down railway station hotel. But the hotelier wouldn't let me let leave so easily. He pulled me aside and offered coffee and cakes in the hotel restaurant. At the house's expense, he stressed.

As soon as I sat down, he spoke softly as to talk to me confidentially. "You'd probably be best served by staying here during Christmas and then just going home again," he said with a worried and almost paternal mine.

But he is probably just trying to get a profit out of it, the longer I stay here in the hotel, I think. But I'm not going to do that. I will just leave as I planned to do. It is high time for that. He must be able to understand that I actually have a fianc é and her family waiting for me, and I'm not going to change my agenda.

He looks almost saddened at me and sighs.

"Very well," he says, "it's your own decision. I can only give you some advice. I'm afraid I have no means of holding you here against your will. We are no longer allowed to do so unless it is the interests of the State that are at stake. But please listen to my advice. Then it is up to you to do what you think is in your best interest. But do not come running back here and say that I haven't warned you. I wish you would think it over once more."

I still maintain my decision. I am impatient to get going. Once again, he shakes his head worriedly, as if he doesn't understand me at all, and then he says:

"Well, do as you please, if you have to. But I suggest that at least you leave your two largest suitcases safely here and just take the weekend bag with you. We'll take good care of the suitcases for you. Then you can always send for them if you decide on a longer stay. If you do, we'll send them anywhere you want."

Maybe that is a good idea. Especially since I have been wanting to take a walk through the city and get some fresh air in the beautiful sunny weather that it has suddenly become. I've been looking at a map of the city, and it doesn't seem that's very far to the neighborhood where my fianc é Julie and her parents live. No longer than you can easily walk there in the good weather. Especially if you don't have two big suitcases to carry. Accordingly, I say yes to his offer. Then I put on my coat and go out on the town, accompanied only by my weekend bag with the most necessary things. I want to see a bit of the city along the way.

A walk in the city

Most of the houses I pass by during my walk appear to be run down and poorly maintained. At least here in the railway station district. It's rather dirty on the streets. There aren't many cars. Mostly Russian and East German cars of older models. There are also some old Skodas. Most people are dressed in clothes where brownish and greyish shades are dominant. It all gives an impression of poverty.

The thick layer of snow that has fallen in previous days is still there in most places. Although in some places it have started to melt. Where there is most sunshine. Only in a few places have the streets been cleared of snow. As I've walked a little, I come through a series of streets with fairly low, older houses, where poorly dressed half-old whores stand in gates and doorways and with loud heckling of themselves to the passing men.

Some of them sound almost like the fruit merchants I know from my hometown. Those who stand on the street with a tow truck with various fruits, apples, oranges and so on, and constantly shout some straps to the passers-by about how good and how cheap their fruits are. The hookers here are even more intrusive. There are hardly any other people on the street, so they are obviously desperate to get some customers. They have probably spotted that I am a more affluent tourist from abroad.

But I consistently say no to the many offers. I am determined that now I will no longer be distracted from my goal. Namely, to get to Julie, who is waiting for me and

surely can't understand why I am not
turning up as promised. And my future in-
laws. But they must know what the
situation is like in this country. With
phones that don't work and everything
else. Still, I'm pretty nervous about
meeting them. It all looks bad.

As I have come a little further away from
the railway station district, I come to some
slightly larger and wider streets. Here there
is more car traffic and quite a few
pedestrians on the streets. It's shopping
streets and people are busy with
Christmas shopping.

It's harder to find your way than I
expected. I have to ask for directions
several times. Many of the slightly larger
streets are similar, as if the houses are
built according to the same drawings and
kept in the same sad colors. Most are
concrete houses in a style that leads the

idea to the old East Germany. I have a feeling that I am going to go some pretty long detours. At least it turns out to be quite a long stroll.

After a long walk around the fairly similar streets and without encountering any churches, town halls, old castles or other sights that could give a little change in the cityscape, I come to a large open square that seems rather windswept.

The entire large space is not paved, but just the gravel deck. Most of it was covered in thin snow. But on the open surfaces it was partially blown away by a fervent wind. Just when I was stopped somewhere on the edge of the great square, it started to snow again. Small hard fluff of frost snow of the type that swirls around in the wind like a whole blizzard when it blows up.

At the other end of the square, a lot of people have gathered. It has also become colder after the sunshine was replaced by grey weather.

At the that end of the square there is an elevation that looks like some kind of a scene. It's in front of it, people have gathered. I'm going to go there to see what's going on. Up on stage stands a young beautiful girl with long blond hair. She seems to be twenty-something. She stares forward with a blunt gaze. It seems like she's been doped with something.

Next to her is a well-dressed middle-aged man talking in a megaphone. He speaks almost like a market caller. He praises the young woman in a slightly exaggerated way and appreciates all her excellent qualities, while she herself just stands and stares absently, without looking at the man or making eye contact with him. She's just standing there passively like a doll. Next to the hyperactive market caller that gesticulates and strikes out with his arms. He doesn't speak to the young girl at all, but only out to the audience in the square through the megaphone.

The man up on stage shames every imaginable detail about her in a way, so I'd get curvy toes if it was me. First her beauty and all her physical merits. Then her great results and top marks come on her study. Then he goes on to praise her helpfulness to her family and her younger siblings and an old sick aunt, and how popular, she is among her peers at the studio and in the volunteer youth organization, where she is an elite member. She has been named best companion of the year, most beautiful young woman and most beautiful young girl by her peers and her teachers and the country's largest newspaper.

The man on the podium repeats it over and over again, in almost the same words. It seems increasingly exaggerated and almost embarrassing every time he repeats it. With all sorts of elaborate details and small concrete examples of how amazing this girl is. Occasionally, in addition to the assembly in the square, he repeatedly shouts whether they agree, and each time the Assembly responds with tactful and increasingly forceful 'yes' cries. It seems like he's trying to whip up a public mood. But why? Why should this particular young girl be hailed and showered with all that praise? She is just standing there on the podium and looks like she's not really there.

The proclamation urges anyone who does not agree, or has any objection to what he says, to object here and now – or to keep quiet about it forever. It sounds like an old-fashioned wedding ritual, where there will be "desire" in the past for the bride and groom in the church, and if anyone objects to doing anything about the marriage, they must come up with it now, or keep quiet about it forever. That's the associations I get on it. It is quite absurd about the situation.

And now he continues to shout beyond the square in his megaphone that if anyone objects to what he has said, then they must be able to justify it beyond any doubt. You must be able to point out that there is another young woman of the same age elsewhere in the country who is more beautiful, wiser, more skilled, more diligent, more helpful and loving about her family and more valued by her teachers and more popular with her peers than her on the podium, who is still completely passive next to him and looks as if she is not at all well in the situation. And if anyone objects, they should be able to provide opinions, pictures and other evidence of it.

He repeats it over and over again, but no one objects. Everyone just stands as mesmerized and looks at him and the girl, and shouts "yes" and other affirmative words every time he asks them. It's a bit like a rock concert where the musicians try to knock the mood of the audience by shouting "are you there?" and similar things to the audience.

But this guy has taken it some steps further, so it seems like a kind of mass hysteria that the announcer is trying to create. And which he apparently succeeds with. He's whipping up a mood and he obviously knows what he's doing. He seems very professional, like someone who knows which buttons he needs to press to elicit a certain effect in the audience, which is now completely up and running with enthusiasm. He has the audience in the palm of his hand. It seems almost creepy to witness when you are not part of it, but just a visiting foreigner from another country.

I still haven't understood *why* the girl should be paid a tribute like that. Is she a pop star, or a movie star, or a sports hero who has set new records, or what? But that's not what the caller says. He does not mention anything of that kind.

When he finally takes a little break, I ask one of the other onlookers what it is all about and why the girl is being hailed and cheered in that way. The first one I ask asks me to repeat it. He probably assumes that everyone knows that. Then he just shrugs his shoulders and rushes away.

A young couple is more welcoming. They have heard my question and give themselves time to explain something about that year's Christmas Queen. Every year, a Christmas Queen is chosen and named, who is hailed and cheered. It's an ancient tradition in that country. It must be the most beautiful and brightest and most accomplished young girl in the whole country. There must be no one else to outshine her.

Once she's named Christmas Queen of the Year, she'll be celebrated and applauded by everyone. Both at public meetings like this, and in all the country's newspapers and radio and television programs, and on the sporadic version of the Internet that exists in this country, where all the media are state-run. In the weeks leading up to Christmas, she is hailed as a movie star or a pop singer. It culminates on Christmas Eve and Christmas Day.

In the evening, she is a guest of honor at a banquet at the city's most expensive and exclusive luxury restaurant, where otherwise only the absolute upper class and high-ranking members of the regime are admitted. This evening, the restaurant is closed to everyone else.

Only the top people of society, secretaries of state, generals, business leaders, the highest party leaders are the only ones permitted, and others at the absolute top of society, are taking part in the great banquet in honor of this year's Christmas Queen. President Augusto Miranka himself has the Christmas Queen at the table and gives a tribute speech to her.

She's the guest of honor. The president's speech will be printed the following day prominently in all of the country's newspapers. The speech is primarily a tribute to her for her personal qualities, and rarely touches on more political issues. Being hailed and praised by the president himself at a banquet like this is considered the greatest honor that can surpass any ordinary citizen of the country, the two sympathetic young people explain. This honor rubs off on her entire family, who in the future may have a number of benefits that are usually not available to ordinary people. It's like a knighthood to all her relatives.

In the days leading up to the banquet, she can go shopping in the city's top shops and buy the most expensive and elegant dresses, shoes, bags, jewelry, and anything else she wants. And it's just the culmination of a whole month in which she lives in the wildest luxury like a movie star. It's like winning a month's life as a princess.

That is what the two young people tell me. The Christmas Queen is photographed in the most elegant dresses for all the country's newspapers and television stations, and she is portrayed as an ideal for all other young girls. For many young women, it is their greatest wish to be named Christmas Queen.

But very few achieve anything like this unimaginable luxury in the poor country, where many find it difficult to cope with life. Only one Christmas Queen is named every year. For most people it's a completely unattainable dream. There have been some unfortunate cases of young girls who were beautiful and talented and everything else, and who were runners-up and close to being named, but who still did not become a Queen of Christmas and who were so disappointed that they tried to kill themselves.

Such traditions are not always just good, the young couple tell me, while they indiscriminately look around and lower their voices. And no one knows what will become of the Christmas Queens later on. The young man hushed his girlfriend and says "not here." To me, he explains in a low-key way that there are agents of the secret police who keep an eye on people everywhere. The two young people ask if I would like to see one of the local taverns and have a good glass of beer.

At the tavern

I follow the two young people through a neighborhood of the city with little crooked streets. The houses are a mix of small provincial town houses, small workshop buildings and old warehouses. They apparently know the way quite well.

We walk in through a gate, in through two backyards, before finally getting to a small cellar staircase down to what from the outside look like a small workshop for a bicycle smith. There are some bicycles for sale in a stand outside and there is a sign above the small shop window where part of the paint is shelled out, but it appears that here you can get your bike repaired. We walk down a small staircase to the shop door. This is where the young girl rings a bell and knocks a signal on the door. A little while later, the door is opened by a man in his thirties who first asks the two young people what kind of guest they have brought – that is, me. After a little explanation about it, we'll be let in. The front room – the storeroom – looks like a normal bicycle workshop of the older date, with old, worn fixtures, with bicycles all around in varying degrees of repair or refurbishment. There are also shelves with equipment and spare parts for bicycles – bicycle lights, luggage racks, bicycle tires and bicycle hoses, bicycle chains, etc.

They lead me through the shop into a room at the back, more reminiscent of an old-fashioned tavern. They carefully close the door and pull out a curtain of some thick fabric so that the sound of people chatting together inside the tavern is muffled. The lights in the bike shop were only turned on when the door was opened and turned off again as soon as we had been soldered into the room behind. I'm not free to think they might seem just legally paranoid. But I don't know the circumstances there.

I'm being benched by a long time away with some of their comrades. They are very interested in talking to someone from one of their neighboring countries. I understand from them that it is not often that they have the opportunity to do so, and the news dissemination there in the country is more marked by the propaganda of the regime than by real information. Many news reports are heavily distorted to fit into the regime's "official views." And not much they are told about conditions in other countries.

The young people around the table are critical of the regime, but go very quietly with it so as not to call upon the attention of the regime. They ask me a lot of questions, both about what the situation is in the country I come from and about international issues.

They also explain to me a little more about that whole show with the Christmas Queen. That's what they call it. A staged show to the people. But at the same time, it is evidently rooted in ancient local traditions, which the young people describe as medieval superstitions.

Almost as if some demons with an obscure four-tie to the mystery of Christmas take care to avoid sabotaging the Christmas wonder and staying calm so that nothing dark and negative happens like murder, violence, family tragedies, excessive drinking and so on during the Festive season – let alone a devastating Christmas storm, earthquake or other disasters. Or violent explosions at the old run-down steel works and factories. Or a lot of miners being locked in the coal mine deep mining corridors, as happened about 20 years ago, just on Christmas Day, just a year when many thought they had started taking too easy on all these things and neglecting the age-old traditions, so that the Christmas sacrifice were close to being reduced it to something only symbolic.

It was the dictator Augusto Miranka himself who, the following year, set tougher and more serious rules for the Christmas sacrifice, which had to be observed to the letter, and since then there have actually been no truly great disasters with many hundreds of people perished – at least not just during the Christmas period, as one of the young people emphasizes.

Another young woman adds that the government should probably rather do much more to ensure working conditions in mines and factories and farms, instead of just relying on age-old kinds of superstition. Because in many places the working conditions and the security of the workers is under all the criticism.

This whole thing with The Christmas Queen serves an ancient ritual to ensure peace and prosperity in the coming year for the run-down industrial city, which is plagued by great poverty, violence, vandalism, prostitution and crime – just like the rest of the country. It's a kind of Christmas sacrifice, they say. The Christmas Queen is given as a sacrifice to the so-called Demons of Christmas, in order to ensure Christmas peace for the rest of the country and the people.

An ancient custom dating back to the Middle Ages or beyond. They describe it to me as a much more violent version of the well-known tradition of firing fireworks on

New Year's Eve in many countries to scare away the demons around the midnight hour at New Year's Eve.

I ask if this is entirely symbolic. No, say, it's quite bloody and concrete. The most beautiful young girl is first feted and hailed and cheered like a movie star, and then she is hung on the shaft in a corner of the square where there is a gallows that is only used for that purpose. While everyone in the city who is able to be present stands in the square and witnesses it, and afterwards goes home to celebrate Christmas in the safe assurance that Christmas peace is once again guaranteed so that Christmas and the next year are not affected by disasters or major accidents caused by the hungry Christmas demons, which have, so to speak, been satisfied once again.

The Christmas Sacrifice, where the Queen
of Christmas is handed over to the
Christmas Demons — as it is official
designated — takes place on the afternoon
of Christmas Eve and has the character of
a big fable. On the other hand, Christmas
Day is a much more quiet and solemn
holiday, mostly celebrated at home with the
immediate family, after attending church
for Christmas and afterwards returning
home for Christmas dinner with one's
family.

All this with the sacrifice of The Christmas
Queen sounds barbaric, I say. It's a kind of
human sacrifice that you read about in
ancient stories. Something from a much
older and more primitive kind of society.
Yes, say the young people. They certainly
agree with me that it is barbaric practice
that should have been abolished a long
time ago. They say they have discussed it
with some of their friends and have talked

about what they can do about it. But it's hard in a dictatorship state as it is. And the dictator himself, Augusto Miranka, plays a central role in it. He is the one who hands her over to the executioner and he uses all that with the terrible superstition of the Christmas Demons, which must be given a human sacrifice in his propaganda to keep the people down, just like his predecessors.

In our era of modern media, it has come to play an even greater role than otherwise. The young people around me lower their voices and say that many radical youths have considered whether they can somehow free the young woman before she is hanged and then get away and hide her somewhere. But it's very difficult because the secret police is everywhere and is overseeing everything and everyone, so the whole thing in the city square is obviously filled with security guards and police officers, so any actions of that kind have been made impossible.

Most people in the city – and in the country – believe that it is these Christmas demons that are to blame for the fact that there is such a massive lot of drinking and violence and fights and even murders and family tragedies during the time of Christmas. It is still a widespread perception in the general population.

This thing with all the extra drinking and family-tragedies and all that kind of things happening at Christmas, you do know something like that in your own country too, they ask me. And I have to agree. But young people around me is convinced that there is a very prosaic explanation for it.

In this country, they say, most people need something to calm them down during the hours of the 24 of December, to calm their nerves that are on edge in the hours up to midnight on Christmas Eve. Because, according to tradition, it is at midnight between the 24 and the 25 of December that the Christmas wonder once again happens – that is, if everything goes well and it is not derailed by the Christmas Demons, that are trying as hard as they can to sabotage it. And you can never know beforehand, whether the sacrifice of the Christmas Queen will be well received by the demons, or that maybe some little thing has gone wrong during the process, so that the demons are not satisfied and will not accept the sacrifice and therefore create a disaster that is feared by everyone in society. That is how it is perceived from the days of old in this country.

The time up to midnight, the last hours up to the point, where the Christmas Wonder takes place once again, are the most vulnerable to the impact of the demons. According to old superstition, it takes only

a tiny bit to overturn or prevent the
Christmas wonder from happening, and
that would be a disaster, for the demons
are lurking to deprive people of the lovely
and miraculous Christmas-luck, which
brings light and joy to men and helps to
sustain the cosmos in the face of the
ever-looming chaos — something like that,
they say, is the way the age-old
superstition explain these matters.

Many people still fear major disasters, such
as a large earthquake that sometimes
happens in this area, or almost the end of
the World, unless there anything is done to
satisfy the Christmas demons. Therefore, a
sacrifice must be made to quiet their
hunger, to satisfy their greed to destroy
something of the most beautiful and lovely
from the human world. And this is done by
selecting the most beautiful and brightest
and most exemplary young girl, first
celebrating her as a Queen of Christmas

and leading her on in every kind of media, and then sacrificing her for the sake of Christmas – to give the demons what they want, so as to make them leave the rest of the world untouched.

Therefore, everyone's nerves are on edge. You can never be quite sure, whether this will be successful, so that the Miracle of Christmas will happen once again. Accordingly, most people are stressed with fear during these hours, where everything is at stake, and soothe their nerves by drinking huge amounts of beer, wine, and liquor until Christmas Night comes, and the world still standing. Everyone holds their breath and soothes their nerves until it finally happens. Then they go on drinking even more to celebrate the wonderful news. Unfortunately, many will be drinking too much and get angry at others. Many will get aggressive and start fights. All the frustrations they have been through during the year, come forward and are released at the expense of others.

On the other hand, Christmas Day is a joyful celebration. Everyone is so happy that the world is still standing, and in this mood, many articulate good wishes like New Year's resolutions to be better towards others, and to improve yourself as a person.

Christmas Day is the highlight of Christmas. A happy and bright party where you express friendship and love for those you care about and give them gifts. And gather with the family to eat the biggest meal and have the biggest and most important feast of the year.

I believe that the young people in this hidden – or almost secret – caf é are all students and clearly belong to the opposition to the regime. They believe it is high time to put an end to the old superstitions that characterize society in many other respects. And most of all, the gross exploitation of women that is taking place.

A very large proportion of the country's women live as a kind of half-prostitutes who has to offer themselves and their sexual services to men in order to have something to live on. And then there are all the full-time prostitutes, they add. There aren't many jobs for women, and they're all poorly paid.

Equality in education and work is almost non-existent, for example. In fact, the greatest economic re-distribution that is taking place in society is due to women's various forms of prostitution. There is a high unemployment rate and lack of social security. But on the other hand there is a fairly large class of men who are party officials in the only permitted party or managers or consultants or engineers or under-assistant managers in the old-fashioned factories and other companies. Often far more than is needed. The wages in these jobs are often high, often four to five times as high as that of an industrial worker – or even more. There is a widespread nepotism that consumes a great deal of the society's money for wages.

This large group of bureaucrats has a high salary, and it is mostly those who are frequent guests of the prostitutes. It is estimated that as much as one third or a quarter of the income of this rather large group somehow ends up with the prostitutes.

The rest of the population lives in great poverty, which would be even greater without the large redistribution of money through the many prostitutes. It is very common for a married man belonging to the large group of unemployed or low-paid people to actually be dependent on the income of his wife through some kind of prostitution, full-time or part-time. without any real pimping. But in very often it is the only way for a family to get a roof over their heads and food on the table and give their children a good upbringing. This is a huge discrimination against women.

Unemployment benefits and social benefits do not exist, so to speak, or are administered, so that only those from the large group of people who in practice benefit from them, when they are exempt-should sometimes be affected by a social event.

But it's hard to do anything about unless the whole system is changed, young people say. Because if the widespread prostitution,

what one self-in factbeery should af
consideration to women, many of the poor
families would end up in poverty and
misery. The only solution is to change the
whole system how this is to be done, they
do not have a solution to it. I see the
despair on the faces of young women when
they explain this to me. I myself am almost
speechless to hear, just miserable the
conditions are.

I mentioned some of my own experiences
at the hotel, with the maid, who told me
that she would be paid if she could not
hand over money to the hotelier in the
morning for sexual services with the
guests. But I couldn't just give her the
money. She insisted that she should have
sex with me, too.

One of the young people explains. That's
because the money she gets from her guest
is only the smallest part of it. There are

73

built-in surveillance cameras in every room – skillfully and very well hidden. Cameras of good quality indeed. So the nocturnal sex acts are all recorded on tape. The tapes are then later edited into a special kind of porn movies, which one of the dictator's many commercial companies has cultivated a large market for abroad. Your night with the maid are probably already out on the export market in a movie of that type – they sneak upon people's sex life, without people knowing it. Otherwise, they'll probably be released and put up for sale just after a couple of weeks, just in the beginning of the new year. It's become a huge market now. About one quarter of the country's exports come from these kinds of things. That is what they tell me.

They go on explaining about the old-fashioned manufacturing industry and the lack of modernization. As a result of this, the country no longer has very many products to export. Foreign countries do not want to buy them because they can make it cheaper or better themselves. As a result, it is a very big part of the social economy that is based on something that has to do with sex and porn industry. It shows how extreme it has become. It is especially in recent decades, during the reign of Augusto Miranka, that it has developed so violently.

But when made these video recordings with me and the maid, I didn't give them any permission to use them. How can they just use them anyway without asking me.

The youngsters couldn't help but laugh. They can hear that I am coming from abroad, they said. But that's just the way it goes in this country. With everything. There are so many things that need to be reformed.

They returned to the sacrifice of the Christmas Queen. It was tomorrow, Christmas Day, that it was going to take place. They told that they had been arguing about whether it could somehow be stopped.

Both to save the girl from a cruel death and to mark a rebellion against the tyranny of government, which was based on age-old superstition and who believed that they could peel and waltz with the population as they wanted.

As a symbol that now was the new times, to make the people realize that it was time to embark on a path other than dictatorship, oppression and superstition. They took a warm approach to the subject, but only had some vague ideas about how it might be possible.

But what does she even mean about it – the Christmas Queen. She must be terrified at the thought of her being so brutally victimized. Never do any of them flee or try to do so. And then there's even someone running for the Christmas Queen of the Year when they know what it's going to end up with.

A young man took the floor. They say they are brainwashed into seeing it as one of the noblest and most beautiful they can do. A huge service they do to the world and theirs loved ones. A selfless act to prevent that the world collapses – according to the old superstition. Maybe it's in a way similar to the religious martyrs who die for a cause or for a religion they believe in. It's hard for the rest of us to understand. But it is whispered that there is a massive indoctrination and brainwashing in this direction. The regime is adept at this. Many people, including young people firmly believe in this kind of things. And once the group of 12 people moving on to the final term is selected, they are naturally exposed to a massive individual brainwashing. It's scary, but that's how things happen under the regime of the dictator.

These are the kind of methods used by the regime. And they're very efficient at that. They are not quite as adept at running factories and steel mills and the country's economy, but they are quite indifferent to that, because they live even in much privileged conditions and with a completely different standard of living from the general population.

The young people continue to talk about the conditions in the country and there in the city, which is the second largest city and a large industrial city with a lot of steel mills and large factories. But they are old-fashioned and inefficient, they pollute heavily and they are no more competitive internationally. The city is ruled by a powerful and almost autocratic mayor who has been in power for over 25 years. He is a close friend and associate of the country's dictator, Augusto Miranka. There is widespread corruption and nepotism. The mayor controls the city with a heavy hand and Miranka's eloquence. There are rumors that he has secured a large fortune for himself at the expense of ordinary people. The mayor is one of the main figures behind the sacrifice of the Christmas Queen, who is also supported by Miranka.

With his populist charisma and brutal exercise of power, the mayor has succeeded in getting many people among the poor and oppressed population to accept things like the sacrifice of the Christmas Queen and other forms of old superstition, which he quite deliberately uses as part of his position of power.

In secret, however, an opposition movement has emerged, especially among young students. But they have to go quietly and work in secret so as not to be arrested by the secret police. A few times there have been popular demonstrations, for example, about the lack of security in the old coal mines, which still supply most of the country's energy.

The security police have developed a technique of spraying a special kind of chemical liquid on the people who are protesting. It contains something like a fast-paced sleeping aid or anesthetic and penetrates the demonstrators' clothes and pacify them, so that they become dull and passive and at the same time very complacent for some days. It is something in the style of the drugs used for drug rape, so that the police can easily arrest them without resisting, and they even willingly will answer all questions when they are questioned, so on the whole, they eagerly cooperate – wooing with the secret police and thus also immediately stabbing their best friends and, moreover, without resistance reveal everything they know.

That is why the demonstrators have started to dress in big plastic raincoats and fasting masks, because the liquid that is sprayed at the demonstrators with a kind of small water cannon cannot penetrate the plastic in the same way as ordinary clothes made by woven fabrics.

In fact, the students have succeeded in making it a popular trend in the population to be wearing large brightly colored plastic rains-coats, when they are outdoors, so it is difficult for the police to determine who are dissidents – and who are just ordinary citizens.

It had gradually gone into the evening and much of what I had been told about the conditions there in the country has shocked me. Especially all that with the Christmas Queen. I thought human sacrifice was something you did once in the darkest ancient times. It couldn't be right that something like that was still going on. But apparently it still did there in this city. The young people I sat with had begun discussing various options to free the poor girl before she was to be sacrificed.

They suddenly start to talk about the fact that, as a foreigner with quite high status, I have more opportunities to succeed. The authorities will not be so wary of a prosperous tourist and, in general, they do not dare to take as hard a hard line with people from other countries as they do towards their own citizens. They suggest that I impersonate an ethnographer or a doctor from the university of my home country and that I think it is very ethnographic and folkloric interesting with this custom that I have heard of, especially all that about the Christmas demons. Of course, I should only refer to it in positive terms, as if I am a nerdy professor who is only interested in the picturesque and unusual phenomenon of such local customs and traditions – as a folklore researcher who examines colorful local customs.

For example, if I ask permission to interview the girl for my research project on exotic Christmas customs, they might allow me to meet her and talk to her – maybe even so I'm alone with her. And then I'm going to have to try to get her out of there, and get up there with her. Then the young people will get a car so we can get out of here.

They start planning it more in detail. They mention, among other things, that the priest who is to give the Queen of

Christmas absolution and, moreover, be her soul mate in the last hours, is old and infirm and has had several heart attacks.

The plan is for me to give him some confection with some strong sleeping aid in it, so he'll pass out, and it looks like he's had another heart attack. In my hometown, I'm a medical student, and here, I should be impersonating a medical doctor and issuing a death certificate on the priest. Then I'll save the unconscious priest in a desk at the back, and then they'll get a coffin and a hearse, because there's an old tradition in town that it's very serious for a person's peace of mind and bliss in the life after death, if the person should die on Christmas Day, that is, in the critical hours before the Christmas break takes place, so that they don't get to experience it. And it is even more serious if it is a clerical person, the young people explain.

Some of the young people will then
procure a hearse as they drive up to the
back entrance, pretending that it is a
hearse for the old priest, with a coffin
large enough to accommodate the very
corpulent priest. In the confusion that has
arisen, I must then have the young girl,
who is the Christmas Queen of the Year,
smuggled out of the back entrance and put
her in the coffin of the hearse, where I too
have to hide myself. Two of the young
people will then impersonate worshippers
who must hurry to retrieve the body of the
priest and arrange for it to be buried
before midnight in accordance with the old
rules and traditions of people who die just
before Christmas. They must under no
circumstances lie dead, but unburied when
Christmas night comes, according to the
old superstition. The old priest, who is still
made unconscious by the sleeping agent
but otherwise unharmed, is still hidden

inside the desk room. So the two false worshippers must manage to convince everyone that it is the priest who is in the coffin and now has to be buried before midnight in a special cemetery in another city reserved for clergy.

The hearse they got is pretty special, but it was the only one they could get hold of at such short notice. It's not really a real hearse, it's an old three-wheeled van they found in an automobile scrapyard and had a black painted. But it is now very common there in the country with old and run-down cars that have to be repaired with parts from other cars, perhaps by a completely different brand. And there are still quite a few of these old three-wheeled vans, which were built at the time of a car factory in East Germany called Barka, but also in West Germany.

This type of car has only one front wheel. The engine is mounted on top of the front wheel itself, so it will turn with the wheel. The engine then pulls the lone front wheel with chain pull in the style of a motorcycle chain. So it's pretty primitive. Originally, it's a one- or two-cylinder two-stroke engine that pulls it – in fact, almost a motorcycle engine. Some of these three-wheeled vans and small trucks actually have a large and long goods box, and so did this one that served as a hearse.

But on the other hand, a much more powerful engine had been fitted to this one by one of the previous owners. Nothing less than a 2.5 liter V-8 engine that had once been picked out of a Czech-built Tatra passenger car. Now the Tatra engine was air-cooled, and this might have made it a little easier to mount on the front wheel, but it was a considerably bigger and heavier case than a small motorcycle engine. But apparently they had managed to make it work, although they had probably also changed a little on the leverage.

They told me that the car had actually been driving like a hearse for many years, with the small original motorcycle engine, but then it had been bought by some speed-happy guy who had built the big V-8 engine on to it and even tuned the engine so that the rather light wagon could be used in the illegal car races that some young people had fun driving on deserted roads at night. It was still painted pitch black and definitely had the look of a hearse, even in a way that looked a bit exaggerated to me.

For the time being, however, the plan appeared to have succeeded. I was supposed to climb out of the coffin again as soon as we got away a little bit, but we find out that we're being pursued by a police car, so apparently someone's been in the middle of it anyway.

The guy sitting at the wheel is going the nail, and we're racing out of the old three-wheeler- which in the standard version is quite slow in the pull-up, but the V-8 engine has made it a real fast runner. But the police car behind us is also speeding up and we will have to drive almost ten hours in a row at the highest speed to drive from them.

There's no way to stop along the way. We have to continue as fast as we can. We actually succeed in getting away from the police cars, that are trying to catch up on us. I thank heaven for the choice of this special and very unorthodox kind of car. In any kind of ordinary hearse or van or a common passenger car, this would not have been possible. I must admit, that this guy is a very competent driver with lots of experience from the illegal car races on deserted country roads late at night.

Finally, we reach the border and can drive in my own country. The guy at the wheel knows some deserted mountain roads in a distant and sparse populated region up in the mountain area on a large part of the border between the two countries, and here he finds a way to cross the border without any kind of control, and to drive safely into my country. And here the police from the dictatorship state have no authority to pursue us.

We're moving on and we're finally coming to my hometown. After a light meal, we go to bed to get a much-needed night's sleep on top of the dramatic events.

Some other books by Henrik Neergaard

MY NIGHTLY WANDERINGS UNDER SHINING STARS AND DARKEN SKY

A novel

A man makes a bet at a damp Christmas get-together. He bet with a female academic that he can write a book, even if he's not intellectual. And then he's going to have to write that book so as not to lose the bet. The book will contain a little of each about big and small experiences from his daily life. And there are also some thoughts and a little bit of philosopher about things and phenomena in the world and in society. Not least the technical developments, where he and some friends are quite sceptical about the self-driving cars, because they like to sit behind the wheel and control their own car. Otherwise it's just going to be a kind of public transport. I wonder, for example, that there is a great deal about a self-driving motorcycle? He himself says that the book is not autofiction – not ordinary autofiction in any case.

THE ITTY BITTY NITTY GRITTY

NON-LITERARY NON-MAGAZINE

Issue no. 1

A collection of poems, prose and short stories. It starts with the White Paper. Then there are the wheels that spins and spins in the night (but don't think to lubricate them with the animals' blood). Poem No. 2. there are houses that are gray. The city's roads – in the town where he grew up, you didn't just go to a patisserie, and certainly not if you like him were born behind a bush in cemeteries. Then there's

some pre-nostalgic writings for hilarious
Christmas parties with belgian beers, flip
buttons and cats that come running in a
completely disorderly way. Then someone
loves books, but her husband would rather
watch football. And then Mom calls and
has a great idea for a very updated version
of Romeo and Juliet.

NEVER FALL IN LOVE WITH A HOOKER

Short stories

THE WOMAN IN THE PINK DRESS

A novel

The protagonist is a younger man who is on the hunt for a girlfriend – and after his father, who divorced his mother many years ago and whom he is now trying to track down after the disagreements that have been. He is lead seriously astray by a very special woman in a very special pink dress, but manages to get back on the track – i.e. trying to find his father. But his father has moved around a lot and when he finally finds his father's address, he is told by the caretaker that he is late, because his father just died a short time ago. The young man goes to the park cemetery to find his father's grave, but is getting lost. When he gets help from Freja, they are thrown out by a grave digger. The young man meets one of his father's acquaintances, who tells him an incredible story that he refuses to take seriously. But something drives him to investigate it further anyway, and then a few things happen that he hadn't even foreseen. Moreover, some evidence suggests that his biological father may be quite different from the one he always thought.

THE SECRET LIFE OF A STUBBORN LETTUCE EATER

A novel

The action takes place in a single day from early morning to late evening.

A peculiar habit is kept hidden.

A lazy office clerk enjoys his lunch – and the new canteen lady.

Husband and wife live at opposite ends of the house.

Someone suddenly discovers his long lost lover in an unexpected place.